HOW BIG IS A PIG?

Clare Beaton

Barefoot Books
Celebrating Art and Story

Some cows are thin; some cows are fat.
But how big is a pig? Can you tell me that?

Some dogs are quick; some dogs are slow.
But how big is a pig? Do you think you know?

Some hens are in; some hens are out.
But how big is a pig? What's this all about?

Some frogs are jumpy; some frogs are still.
But how big is a pig? Tell me if you will!

Some cats are wild; some cats are tame.
But how big is a pig? Are they all the same?

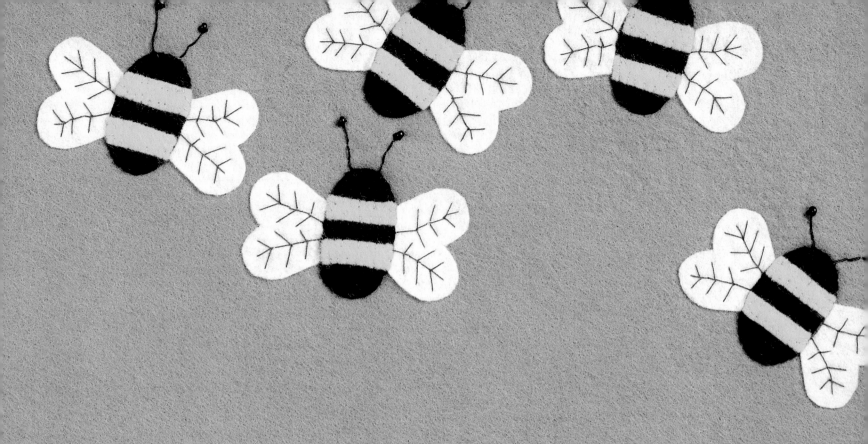

Some bees fly high; some bees fly low.
But how big is a pig? Tell me if you know!

Some geese are dirty; some geese are clean.
But how big is a pig? How many have you seen?

Some horses are young; some horses are old.
But how big is a pig? Have you been told?

Some sheep are black; some sheep are white.
But how big is a pig? Can you answer right?

Some pigs are big; some pigs are small...

...but this pig is my mama and she's the biggest of us all!

Clare Beaton is also the illustrator of *One Moose, Twenty Mice*, *Zoë and her Zebra* and *Mother Goose Remembers*, all published by Barefoot Books.

Praise for *One Moose, Twenty Mice*:

"The illustrations are comfortably tactile and they offer some clever effects...
Young viewers will find the fuzzy menagerie endearing, and they'll giggle
through the rollicking kitty hunt" — *Bulletin of the Center for Children's Books*

"The simple satisfaction of playing the game and the pleasure of the illustrations
guarantee that this counting book will hold children's interest longer than
most. A good participation book for nursery school story hour" — *Booklist*

For my younger son, Tom – C. B.

Barefoot Books
2067 Massachusetts Avenue
Cambridge MA 02140

Text copyright © 2000 by Stella Blackstone
Illustrations copyright © 2000 by Clare Beaton
The moral right of Stella Blackstone to be identified as the
author and Clare Beaton to be identified as the illustrator
of this work has been asserted

This book has been printed on 100% acid-free paper
This book was typeset in Plantin Schoolbook Bold 20 on 28 point
The illustrations were prepared in felt with braid, beads and sequins
Graphic design by Judy Linard, England
Color transparencies by Jonathan Fisher Photography, England
Color separation by Grafiscan, Italy
Printed and bound in China by PrintPlus Ltd.

5 7 9 8 6 4
The Library of Congress cataloged the first paperback edition as follows:
Blackstone, Stella.
    How big is a pig? / Stella Blackstone ; [illustrated by] Clare Beaton.
        p. cm.
    Summary: Contrasts animals in the barnyard, including clean and dirty
geese, fat and thin cows, and big and small pigs.
    ISBN 1-84148-077-0 (pbk. : alk. paper)
    [1. Domestic animals--Fiction. 2. English language--Synonyms and
antonyms--Fiction. 3. Animals--Fiction. 4. Stories in rhyme.] I. Beaton,
Clare, ill. II. Title.
    PZ8.3.B5735How 2006

[E]--dc22

2005022103